"This Land Is Your Land"
Let's Explore the West

Jill C. Wheeler

BATTLE GROUND ACADEMY
Franklin, Tennessee

Published by Abdo & Daughters, 4940 Viking Drive, Suite 622, Edina, MN 55435.

Library bound edition distributed by Rockbottom Books, Pentagon Tower, P.O. Box 36036, Minneapolis, Minnesota 55435.

Copyright ©1994 by Abdo Consulting Group, Inc., Pentagon Tower, P.O. Box 36036, Minneapolis, Minnesota 55435. International copyrights reserved in all countries. No part of this book may be reproduced in any form without written permission from the publisher. Printed in the United States.

Library of Congress Number: 94-12498

Photos by:
Bettmann Archives: 4, 6, 7, 8, 9, 15, 16, 17, 18, 19
Archive Photos: 7
Wide World Photos: 21, 23
John Hamilton: 2, 4, 5, 10, 11, 12, 13, 14, 15

Edited By: John Hamilton

Library of Congress Cataloging–in–Publication Data
Wheeler, Jill C., 1964-
    The Northeast / Jill C. Wheeler
        p.   cm — (America, this land is your land)
    Includes bibliographical references and index.
    ISBN 1-56239-298-0
    1. West (U. S.)--Juvenile Literature. [1. West (U. S.)]
 I. Title. II. Series: Wheeler Jill C. 1964-   America, this land is your land
F591.W66   1994
978—dc20   94-12498
                                    CIP
                                    AC

Contents

Let's Explore The West 4

Historical Highlights 6

Lay Of The Land 10

Plants & Animals 14

Famous Folks 16

Favorite Cities 20

Fast Facts 24

Suggestions For Further Reading 29

Glossary 30

Index 32

◀ Yellowstone Falls in Yellowstone National Park, Wyoming.

Let's Explore the West

▲ *Sunrise over Lake Yellowstone in the Absaroka Range, part of the Rocky Mountains.*

What do you think of when you think of the West? Cowboys and Native Americans? Covered wagons crossing *prairies* and mountain ranges? Farmers and gold miners?

The West is all of that and more. It combines a colorful history and a successful present. Its mountains and deserts are millions of years old. Yet European settlers have lived there less than 200 years.

Much of the West joined the United States in 1803. This was the *Louisiana Purchase*. After U.S. leaders

▲ *Heading west in a covered wagon.*

4

bought the land from France, they wanted it explored. They chose two men for the task. Their names were Meriwether Lewis and William Clark. These men and their party explored this new land. They sent back news on what they found.

Lewis and Clark's reports caused excitement. Thousands of people wanted to live in this new land. They began the journey west. The journey was hard and the new land was harsh. Winters were bitter cold and snowy. Mountains made traveling hard.

These settlers found many special things in the West. Some discovered gold and silver. Others found fertile farmland. Native Americans thought the settlers were trying to take away their homeland. They fought back. Many people died on both sides of these battles.

▲ *Mount Rushmore towers over South Dakota's Black Hills.*

The modern West is still a land of adventure and promise. Rugged mountains attract thousands of visitors each year. Farmers have tamed the fertile plains to produce food. Cities offer a high quality of life for millions of people.

Our journey across the West covers many areas. The plains on the eastern side give way to the majestic Rocky Mountains. To the south, the brilliant desert takes over. Throughout are great rivers and bountiful natural resources. These include timber and *minerals*.

It is easy to see why settlers came to this land of plenty. Let's see how the West has changed since the first Europeans saw its wonders.

◀ *A rainbow shines over the Rockies.*

Historical Highlights

We think of the West as a new land. Yet people have lived there for thousands of years. Native Americans were the first residents of the West. They lived in many different tribes. Then Europeans discovered the land. The European settlers wanted the land for themselves. Following are highlights of this struggle for the West. These events also show how the West has grown and changed.

▲ *Sacajawea, a Native American guide, helps Lewis and Clark explore the West.*

950-1200 The *Pueblo* people of New Mexico thrive.

1540-1542 Spanish explorer Francisco Vásquez de Coronado leads a group of explorers. They visit New Mexico, Kansas and Oklahoma. They are looking for gold.

1610 Spaniard Pedro de Peralta founds Santa Fe, New Mexico. It becomes the oldest state capital in the U.S.

1679 Explorer Daniel Greysolon visits what is now Minnesota. He is the first known European to visit the area.

1706 Spaniard Francisco Cuervo y Valdes founds Albuquerque, New Mexico.

1741 French brothers Francis and Louis Verendrye visit Montana.

1803 The Louisiana Purchase expands U.S. lands. The purchase includes parts of all Western states.

1805 Explorers Meriwether Lewis and William Clark discover a special place. It is where three rivers meet. This is the source of the Missouri River.

1806 Explorer Zebulon Pike discovers a mountain in Colorado. He names it Pikes Peak.

1807 Explorer John Colter discovers Yellowstone and the Tetons.

1822 Captain W.H. Becknell pioneers the *Santa Fe Trail*. Thousands of wagons use the trail to cross Kansas.

1830-1844 U.S. soldiers begin forcing Native Americans off their lands. People call the tribes the Five Civilized Tribes. Soldiers send the people to Oklahoma.

◀ *A Pueblo Indian dancer.*

▼ *Native Americans attack a wagon train heading across the plains.*

1832 Henry Schoolcraft discovers the source of the Mississippi River. He names it Lake Itasca. William Bent finishes building Fort Bent, Colorado. The fort's walls are up to four feet thick. The fort becomes a trade center.

1834 The U.S. government creates *Indian Territory* in Oklahoma. Soldiers send thousands of Native Americans there against their will.

1837 Montana settlers bring a *smallpox epidemic* to local Native Americans. Blankets carry the disease.

1846 U.S. soldiers bring New Mexico under U.S. control. This is during the Mexican War.

1846-47 Thousands of *Mormons* cross Nebraska. They are on their way to Utah.

1848 Spain gives New Mexico to the U.S. The U.S. takes western Colorado in the Mexican War.

1854 The Kansas-Nebraska Act opens these states to settlement. Settlers must decide whether or not they will allow slavery. Many people fight over this issue.

1858 William Larimer and his son found Denver.

1859 *Prospectors* find gold at Gregory Gulch in Colorado. The area becomes Central City.

1860 Prospectors discover gold at Leadville, Colorado.

1861 The government organizes Dakota Territory.

1862 A Nebraskan gets land under the Homestead Act. He is the first in the nation. Soldiers put down an uprising of Sioux Indians in Minnesota. Afterwards, the government hangs 37 Sioux. This is the largest mass execution in U.S. history.

1863 Confederate soldiers attack Lawrence, Kansas. They kill 150 innocent people.

1864 A group of soldiers kills many Native Americans in Colorado. The soldiers are angry because the Native Americans killed some settlers. This is the Battle of Sand Creek.

1868 Government and Native American leaders sign the Laramie Treaty. The treaty ends Chief Red Cloud's War in Wyoming.

1872 Yellowstone becomes the first national park.

1874 General George Custer's party discovers gold in South Dakota. This leads to a gold rush in the Black Hills.

◀ *The Dust Bowl period between 1933 and 1936 caused many families to lose their farms.*

◀ *Testing an atomic bomb in the desert.*

1876 Native Americans defeat General George Custer at the Battle of the Little Big Horn. The fight takes place in eastern Montana. Sitting Bull and Crazy Horse lead the Native American forces.

1877 Prospectors discover silver in Leadville, Colorado. Nez Perce Chief Joseph surrenders to U.S. soldiers. In Nebraska, U.S. soldiers kill Chief Crazy Horse.

1885 The Cherokee build the first telephone line in Oklahoma.

1886 Apache leader Geronimo surrenders to U.S. soldiers. The surrender ends years of warfare between soldiers and Native Americans.

1888 Terrible prairie fires sweep North Dakota.

1889 The government opens unassigned lands to settlement. Ten thousand people move to Oklahoma City in one day.

1890 U.S. soldiers kill more than 200 Native Americans. The massacre takes place at Wounded Knee.

1901 A cowboy discovers a huge hole in the ground. The hole is Carlsbad Caverns in New Mexico.

1916 Mexican revolutionary Pancho Villa crosses the U.S. border. He raids Columbus, New Mexico.

1927 Sculptor Gutzon Borglum begins work. He is carving Mount Rushmore in South Dakota.

1929 Workers build a bridge across Royal Gorge in Colorado. This is the world's largest suspension bridge.

1932 The U.S. and Canada create the International Peace Park. The U.S. calls its part Glacier National Park.

1933-36 A terrible drought hits the West. People call the land the *Dust Bowl*. Thousands of farmers lose their farms.

1942 Soldiers order thousands of Japanese Americans to go to Grenada, Colorado. U.S. leaders fear they might harm the nation's war effort against Japan. The fears prove unnecessary.

1945 Scientists explode the first atomic bomb. The explosion takes place at Trinity Site, New Mexico.

1959 An earthquake creates Montana's Earthquake Lake.

1973 A flood in Rapid City, South Dakota, kills nearly 250 people.

1980 The U.S. Supreme Court orders the government to pay the Sioux tribe of South Dakota. The $122 million payment is for Sioux lands the government took in 1877.

9

Lay of the Land

The landscape of the West changes greatly from east to west. Throughout are some of the nation's most amazing sites.

On the eastern edge, Minnesota is home to thousands of lakes carved by *glaciers*. Pine forests cover northern Minnesota. The forests give way to the plains in the south. The plains stretch across the Dakotas, Nebraska, Kansas and Oklahoma. Farmers have tamed these once wild prairies.

The western Dakotas are where the plains begin to change. The famous Badlands are here. Winds and

▼ *Minnesota, land of 10,000 lakes.*

▲ *The badlands of North and South Dakota create an eerie landscape.*

The Great Plains stretch across the Dakotas, Nebraska, Kansas and Oklahoma. ▶

water carved the rocky cliffs and buttes of the Badlands. Minerals add surprising color. Farther west are the Black Hills of South Dakota. The name comes from the thick forests covering the hills.

Beyond the Dakotas, the Rocky Mountains rise from the plains. These are the highest mountains in the U.S. The *Continental Divide* is in the middle of the mountains. Rivers flowing east of the Divide empty into the Gulf of Mexico or the Atlantic Ocean. Rivers flowing west of the Divide empty into the Pacific Ocean.

◀ *Wildflowers dot a meadow in Glacier National Park, Montana.*

Pipestone National Monument in Minnesota is the only place in the world with this soft red stone. Local Native Americans used the stone to carve peace pipes.

Carlsbad Caverns National Park is a series of huge limestone caves in New Mexico. The caves feature amazing rock formations. One of the chambers is 4,000 feet long. Many bats live here. Visitors gather to watch the bats leave at dusk.

The **Black Hills** and **Badlands** are in South Dakota. The Badlands are dry, rocky hills and bluffs carved by wind and water. Forests cover the Black Hills. The Black Hills are the sacred lands of the Sioux tribe of Native Americans. The world's largest gold mine, Homestead Mine, is here.

The Rockies are different farther south. Snowy peaks change into desert mountains. Seas of sand dunes shift across the land.

Across the West, there is plenty to see. Some highlights include:

The **Garden of the Gods** is a 700-acre park near Colorado Springs, Colorado. Giant red sandstone formations fill the park. Local Native Americans believed the formations once were giants.

Natural wonders fill **Yellowstone National Park**. The park is in Wyoming, Idaho and Montana. It is home to Old Faithful *geyser*. Old Faithful spouts steam high into the air every 50 to 80 minutes. Many unusual animals live here, too.

12

The **Grand Tetons** rise above the plains of western Wyoming. These snow-covered peaks are incredible to see. The highest peak is Grand Teton. It rises 13,770 feet above sea level.

Cheyenne Bottoms is a 41,000-acre *marshland* near Great Bend, Kansas. The marsh attracts millions of birds each year. The birds stop at the marsh during their *migration*. The marsh provides food and a place to rest for these birds. Birds that stop here include the white-rumped sandpiper and the endangered whooping crane.

▲ *The snowy peaks of the Grand Teton Mountains in western Wyoming.*

▼ *Old Faithful geyser erupts in Yellowstone National Park, Wyoming.*

Plants & Animals

The Western landscape varies greatly from Minnesota to Montana. It's not surprising that the plants and animals in this region vary, too.

The woods of Minnesota are home to black bears, white-tail deer, timber wolves and moose. Northern lakes are home to game fish like walleye, northern pike and trout. In the southern part of the state, there are many typical prairie animals. These include gophers, foxes, raccoons and rabbits. Beaver and muskrats live near the rivers and streams.

▲ *A lone bison roams the prairie.*
Wild sunflowers are a common sight. ▲

As the prairie expands west and south, there are even more animals. In Kansas and Oklahoma, you can find prairie dogs, coyotes and armadillos. On the eastern edge of this region, there are hills with pine, pecan, walnut and oak trees. Wildflowers like the prairie rose, coneflower and Indian paintbrush add color to the landscape.

▲ *Cactus.*

▲ *Pronghorn seek food on the prairie.*
◀ *A coyote hunts for dinner.*

▲ *A bighorn sheep at home in the mountains.*

Farther west, farmland covers land that once grew nothing but tall prairie grass. This area is a favorite place for hunters. There are many white-tailed deer and ring-necked pheasants here. The animals feast on wild chokecherries, highbush cranberries and wild plums. Huge herds of buffalo once lived on this land, too. Hunters nearly killed them all in the late 1800s. Visitors can see some smaller herds today.

As you approach the Rocky Mountains, the plants and animals change once more. In the foothills, look for mule deer, pronghorn antelope and jackrabbits. Cottonwoods grow on river banks. Sunflowers and wildflowers wave in the wind. Higher in the mountains, mountain goats, elk and bighorn sheep travel the craggy peaks. They are surrounded by Douglas firs, yellow pines and blue spruce.

These give the mountains their rich green color. The Rockies also are home to an occasional grizzly bear.

The southern part of this region is different still. New Mexico is home to many varieties of cacti and desert animals. Cacti include the prickly pear, the cholla and mesquite. Heat-loving desert animals include rattlesnakes, horned toads and poisonous spiders. The speedy roadrunner is New Mexico's state bird. Sandhill cranes also thrive in New Mexico.

▲ *A rattlesnake, coiled and ready to strike.*

Prairie dogs ▶ *emerge from their underground home.*

Famous Folks

The people of the modern West reflect the area's history. Many residents are of Native American descent. Others have a Mexican heritage. Still others trace ancestors back to Europe. Spanish is a common language in many areas.

All of these early residents share a common trait. They were willing to work hard. We see the results of their work today. Some of these people became famous through their efforts. Following are profiles of a few of them.

William Harrison "Jack" Dempsey (1895–1984) Dempsey was the most popular heavyweight boxer of all time. He was born in Manassa, Colorado. He held the World Heavyweight title from 1919 to 1926.

Judy Garland (1922–1969) This singer/actress played Dorothy in "The Wizard of Oz." She was born in Grand Rapids, Minnesota. She also starred in many other films.

Henry John "John Denver" Deutschendorf (1943–) This popular singer was born in Roswell, New Mexico. He changed his name to the name of one of his favorite cities.

Walter Percy Chrysler (1875–1940) Chrysler was a successful car maker. He started the Chrysler Corporation in 1925. He was from Wamego, Kansas.

F. Scott Fitzgerald (1896–1940) This author is best known for writing *The Great Gatsby*. The book told about life in the 1920s. Fitzgerald wrote many other books, too. He lived in St. Paul, Minnesota.

Amelia Mary Earhart (1897–1937) Earhart was a famous airplane pilot. She was born in Atchison, Kansas. She became the first woman to fly across the Atlantic Ocean. In 1937, she tried to fly around the world. Her plane was lost during the trip. No one is sure what happened to her.

William James Mayo (1861–1939) & **Charles Horace Mayo** (1865–1939). These Minnesota brothers founded the world-famous Mayo Clinic in Rochester, Minnesota. Their research helped more people recover from operations.

Charles Monroe Schultz (1922–) Schultz created the Peanuts cartoon strip. He was born in Minneapolis, Minnesota. His characters still delight people today.

Sacajawea (1787?–1812?) Sacajawea was a Shoshone Indian woman. She married a French trader. She served as a guide on the Lewis and Clark expedition. She probably was born in western Montana.

Jeannette Rankin (1880–1973) Rankin was the first woman elected to the U.S. Congress. She worked to improve the lives of poor women and their children. She was born in Missoula, Montana.

Fred Astaire (1899–1987) This famous dancer and singer was born in Omaha, Nebraska. He gained fame dancing with Ginger Rogers. He received a special Academy Award in 1949 for his work.

Gerald Ford (1913–) The nation's 38th president, Ford was born in Omaha, Nebraska. He served as vice president under Richard Nixon. Ford spent 25 years in Congress. Before that, he worked as a coach and also a lawyer.

Marlon Brando (1924–) Brando is one of the nation's most successful actors. He is best known for roles in "A Streetcar named Desire" and "The Godfather." He was born in Omaha, Nebraska.

Henry Fonda (1905–1982) Fonda was a successful stage and screen actor. He starred in comedies and dramas. His movies included "The Grapes of Wrath" and "On Golden Pond." His children Jane and Peter also are actors. Fonda was born in Grand Island, Nebraska.

Malcolm X (1925–1965) This famous African-American leader was born in Omaha, Nebraska. He worked to help African-Americans gain equal power to whites. He studied Islam while in prison and became a spokesperson for the Black Muslim movement. Assassins killed him in New York City.

Demi Moore (1962–) This popular actress is from Roswell, New Mexico. She has starred in many movies, including "Ghost."

Lawrence Welk (1903–1992) Millions of people have enjoyed the music of this famous bandleader. He was a native of Strasburg, North Dakota. He had his own television show for many years.

Mickey Mantle (1931–) Mantle was born in Spavinaw, Oklahoma. This famous baseball player hit 536 home runs in his career. He joined the Baseball Hall of Fame in 1974.

Oral Roberts (1918–) Roberts gained fame as preacher on television. He founded Oral Roberts University in Tulsa, Oklahoma. He was born in Ada, Oklahoma.

Will Rogers (1879–1935) Rogers was a world-famous actor, writer and comedian. He was from Ooligah,

Oklahoma and was part Cherokee. He died in a plane crash in Alaska.

James Francis "Jim" Thorpe (1888–1953) Thorpe was a Native American of the Sauk and Fox tribe. Some people called him the world's greatest athlete. He won Olympic gold medals and played professional football. He was born in Prague, Oklahoma.

Crazy Horse (1849?–1877) This chief of the Oglala Sioux tribe fought the U.S. Cavalry. He did not want his people moved to a *reservation*. Crazy Horse led Native American warriors in the Battle of the Little Big Horn. He was born in South Dakota.

Red Cloud (1822–1909) Red Cloud was head chief of the Oglala Lakota Sioux tribe. He fought U.S. soldiers from 1859 to 1868. He wanted to keep white settlers from Native American lands. In 1868, he signed a peace treaty. He spent the rest of his life on a reservation.

Sitting Bull (1831?–1890) Sitting Bull was a chief of the Hunkpapa Sioux tribe. He also was a medicine man. He helped defeat General Custer at the Battle of the Little Big Horn. Sitting Bull was born in South Dakota. ▼

Favorite Cities

Cities are not as common in the West as in other parts of the nation. Many people in the West live in rural areas. Yet there are a few cities that play an important role in the region's success.

Albuquerque

Albuquerque, New Mexico, sits on the Rio Grande River. City *factories* make truck trailers, electronic equipment and aerospace parts. The city also has mining, timber and ranching operations.

The Spanish founded Albuquerque in 1706. The U.S. Army built a fort there in 1846. *Confederate* forces captured the city during the Civil War. Yet residents remained loyal to the U.S. through the war.

Today, Albuquerque hosts the annual International Balloon Fiesta. This colorful event attracts many visitors.

Billings

Billings, Montana, is Montana's largest city. It is on the Yellowstone River. Agriculture is important to Billings. Local farmers produce sugar beets, cattle and sheep. In the city, industries include oil refining, meat packing and flour milling.

Billings began in 1882. The Northern Pacific Railway started the city. Railroad officials named the city after the railroad's president. His name was Frederick Billings.

Nearby is Custer Battlefield National Monument. Here, visitors can explore the famous battle sites along the Little Big Horn River.

Denver

People call **Denver, Colorado,** the Mile High City. It sits one mile above sea level. It is the capital of Colorado. The Rocky Mountains rise to the west of Denver.

▲ *A skyline view of Denver, Colorado.*

Denver's key industries are sales and distribution. The city also is a gateway to Rocky Mountain attractions. Denver is home to a branch of the U.S. Mint. Visitors may also visit the Colorado State Historical Museum and the Denver Art Museum.

The city began in 1860 with two small mining camps. The coming of the railroad and a silver-mining boom both helped the city grow quickly. Today, Denver is the main urban center between Minneapolis and the Pacific Coast.

Kansas City

Kansas City, Kansas, sprawls on either side of the Kansas River. It is where the Kansas River meets the Missouri River. Kansas City is in both Kansas and Missouri. The city became a transportation hub in 1869. That year, workers built the first bridge across the Missouri River.

Agriculture is very important to Kansas City. The city has the world's largest grain elevator. At other factories, workers process meat, mill flour and make cars. Kansas City also is home to the Nelson-Atkins Museum of Art. It is one of the nation's leading art museums. Visitors can enjoy horse racing and dog racing at local tracks.

The city began in 1821. It started as a trading post. In 1981, a disaster at a Kansas City hotel killed more than 100 people. The city also suffered during floods in 1993.

Oklahoma City

Oklahoma City, Oklahoma, is the capital of Oklahoma. It is the state's largest city. Oil is a vital industry. The Capitol building sits on an oil field. Oil is pumped out from under the Capitol grounds. Oil derricks highlight the city skyline.

Aerospace is a major industry in Oklahoma City. The city is home to Tinker Air Force Base and the Federal Aviation Agency Aeronautical Center. Other businesses process and ship livestock and grain products.

Visitors to Oklahoma can see the National Cowboy Hall of Fame and the Western Heritage Center. A symphony and several theater companies provide other attractions.

Oklahoma City was settled in one day. On April 22, 1889, the government opened the area for settlement. Nearly 10,000 people flocked to the city that day.

Omaha

Omaha, Nebraska, sits on the Missouri River. It is the state's largest city. It is a major center for rail, trade, insurance, and food processing.

Omaha Indians lived on the city's land until 1854. Then, the government opened Nebraska Territory for settlement. The city grew rapidly during the westward expansion. Settlers would stop in Omaha to buy supplies before heading west.

The first transcontinental railroad arrived in Omaha in 1865. It was the Union Pacific. The railroad company built stockyards in Omaha in the 1880s. This started the city's livestock marketing and processing industry.

▲ *Minneapolis glows at night.*

Minneapolis

Minneapolis, Minnesota, is the largest city in the state. Together with St. Paul, it forms the Twin Cities. Minneapolis is a cultural center for this region. It is home to the Minneapolis Institute of Arts, as well as the famous Guthrie Theater.

Minneapolis grew up around Fort Snelling. The fort was built in 1819 where the Mississippi and Minnesota rivers meet. The Mississippi River helped local businesses. Its falls made power for a grain milling industry. This industry used grain produced by farmers. Minneapolis became known as "Mill City." The city still is home to food companies General Mills and Pillsbury.

Minneapolis is still an important city for agriculture. The Minneapolis Grain Exchange is located here. The University of Minnesota still conducts important agricultural research. Other industries include printing and publishing, computers and food processing.

Fast Facts

Colorado
Population: 3.3 million
Area: 104,091 square miles
Capital: Denver
Industries: Aerospace, agriculture, electronics, manufacturing, mining, tourism.
State Flower: Rocky Mountain columbine
State Bird: Lark bunting
Statehood Date: August 1, 1876

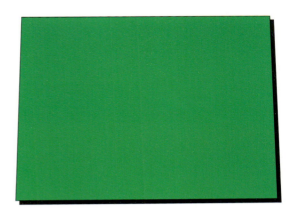

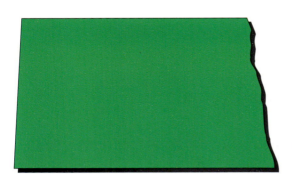

North Dakota
Population: 640,000
Area: 70,702 square miles
Capital: Bismarck
Industries: Agriculture, farm machinery, livestock, mining.
State Flower: Wild prairie rose
State Bird: Western meadowlark
Statehood Date: November 1, 1889

South Dakota

Population: 700,000
Area: 77,116 square miles
Capital: Pierre
Industries: Agriculture, food processing, manufacturing.
State Flower: Pasqueflower
State Bird: Ring-necked pheasant
Statehood Date: November 2, 1889

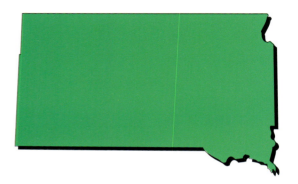

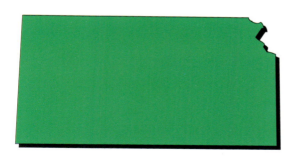

Kansas

Population: 2.5 million
Area: 82,277 square miles
Capital: Topeka
Industries: Agriculture, manufacturing, printing and publishing.
State Flower: Native sunflower
State Bird: Western meadowlark
Statehood Date: January 19, 1861

Minnesota

Population: 4.4 million
Area: 84,402 square miles
Capital: St. Paul
Industries: Agriculture, chemicals, fishing, mining, manufacturing.
State Flower: Pink and white lady's slipper
State Bird: Common loon
Statehood Date: May 11, 1858

Montana

Population: 800,000
Area: 147,046 square miles
Capital: Helena
Industries: Agriculture, lumber, oil and gas, silver and copper mining and smelting.
State Flower: Bitterroot
State Bird: Western meadowlark
Statehood Date: November 8, 1889

Nebraska

Population: 1.6 million
Area: 77,355 square miles
Capital: Lincoln
Industries: Aerospace, agriculture, food processing, manufacturing, metal products.
State Flower: Goldenrod
State Bird: Western meadowlark
Statehood Date: March 1, 1867

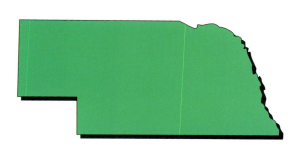

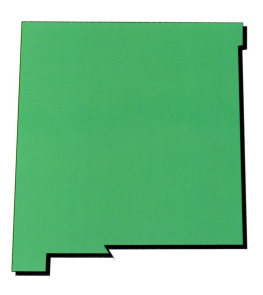

New Mexico

Population: 1.5 million
Area: 121,593 square miles
Capital: Santa Fe
Industries: Agriculture, lumber, machinery, minerals, printing, research, tourism.
State Flower: Yucca
State Bird: Roadrunner
Statehood Date: January 6, 1912

Oklahoma

Population: 3.1 million
Area: 69,919 square miles
Capital: Oklahoma City
Industries: Agriculture, manufacturing, mineral and energy exploration and production, printing and publishing.
State Flower: Mistletoe
State Bird: Scissor-tailed flycatcher
Statehood Date: November 16, 1907

Wyoming

Population: 450,000
Area: 97,809 square miles
Capital: Cheyenne
Industries: Agriculture, clay and glass products, mining, tourism, wood products.
State Flower: Indian paintbrush
State Bird: Meadowlark
Statehood Date: July 10, 1890

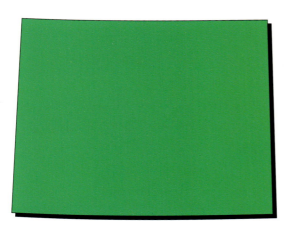

Suggestions For Further Reading

Kids Learn America by Patricia Gordon and Reed C. Snow, Williamsburg Publishing Co.

Children's Atlas of the United States, Rand McNally & Company.

All About Our 50 States by Margaret Ronan, Random House.

Going West: Cowboys and Pioneers by Martine Courtault, Marboro Books.

Children of the Wild West by Russell Freedman, Clarion Books.

The World's Great Explorers — Meriwether Lewis and William Clark by Christine A. Fitz-Gerald, Childrens Press.

Glossary

Confederate
Name given to the Southern states during the United States Civil War.

Continental Divide
A line of mountain peaks. Rivers to the east of the peaks flow toward the Atlantic Ocean. Rivers to the west flow to the Pacific Ocean.

Dust Bowl
An area that suffered from long dry spells and dust storms. This happened most in the 1930s.

Epidemic
When many people are sick at the same time.

Factories
Places where people make products.

Five Civilized Tribes
Five tribes of Native Americans who lived much like European settlers. The government forced them to live in Oklahoma.

Geyser
A spring that shoots up hot water and steam.

Glacier
A mass of slowly moving ice.

Homestead Act
A law passed by Congress in 1862. It gave each settler 160 acres of land. The settler had to live on the land and farm it.

Indian Territory
Land in part of Nebraska, Kansas and Oklahoma. The government forced Native Americans to live on this land in the 1800s.

Louisiana Purchase
A large territory west of the Mississippi River. The United States bought the land from France in 1803.

Marshland
A spongy wetland soaked with water for long periods of time.

Mormons
People who practice the Mormon religion.

Prairies
A large area of level or gently rolling grassy land with few trees.

Prospectors
People who looked for gold and other minerals.

Pueblo
An Indian tribe that lived in the West many years ago.

Reservation
A place where the government sent Native Americans to live.

Santa Fe Trail
A route followed by settlers going west. It ran from Independence, Missouri, to Santa Fe, New Mexico.

Smallpox
A deadly disease.

Index

A
Albuquerque, NM   20
Armadillos   14
Astaire, Fred   17

B
Badlands   10, 11, 12
Bighorn sheep   15
Billings, MT   20
Black bear   14
Black Hills   5, 8, 11, 12
Brando, Marlon   18
Buffalo   15

C
Carlsbad Caverns National
    Park   12
Cheyenne Bottoms   13
Chrysler, Walter Percy   16
Clark, William   5, 6, 29
Continental Divide   11, 30
Cottonwood   15
Coyotes   14
Crazy Horse   9, 19

D
Dallas   21
Dempsey, "Jack"   16
Denver, Colorado   20, 21
Denver, John   16
Dust Bowl   8, 9, 30

E
Earhart, Amelia Mary   17

F
Fitzgerald, F. Scott   16
Fonda, Henry   18
Ford, Gerald   17

G
Garden of the Gods   12
Garland, Judy   16
Geyser   12, 13, 30
Glacier   9, 10, 12, 30
Glacier National Park   9, 12
Grand Tetons   13
Grizzly bear   15

I
Indian paintbrush   14, 28

K
Kansas City, KS   21

L
Lewis, Meriwether   5, 6, 29
Louisiana Purchase   5, 6, 31

M
Mantle, Mickey   18
Mayo, Charles Horace   17
Mayo, William James   17
Minneapolis, MN   17, 23
Moore, Demi   18
Moose   14
Mount Rushmore   5, 9

N
Northern pike   14

O
Oklahoma City, OK   22
Old Faithful   12, 13
Omaha, NE   17, 18, 22

P
Pipestone National
    Monument   12
Plains   5, 7, 10, 11, 13

Prairie   4, 9, 10, 15, 24, 31
Prairie dogs   14, 15
Prairie grass   15
Prairie rose   14, 24

R
Rankin, Jeannette   17
Red Cloud   8, 19
Roadrunner   15, 27
Roberts, Oral   18
Rocky Mountains   4, 5, 11,
    15, 20
Rogers, Will   18

S
Sacajawea   6, 17
Schultz, Charles Monroe   17
Sioux   8, 9, 12, 19
Sitting Bull   9, 19
Sunflowers   14, 15

T
Thorpe, "Jim"   19
Timber wolves   14

W
Walleye   14
Welk, Lawrence   18

X
X, Malcolm   18

Y
Yellowstone National
    Park   3, 12, 13

978
Whe

9061

Wheeler, Jill C.
    Let's explore the
west